The Three

D1451414

Cover illustrated by	Adapted by	Illustrated by
Deborah Colvin Borgo	Sarah Toast	Susan Spellman

Louis Weber, C.E.O.
Publications International, Ltd.
7373 North Cicero Avenue
Lincolnwood, Illinois 60646

Manufactured in U.S.A.

8 7 6 5 4 3 2 1

ISBN: 0-7853-1851-8

Publications International, Ltd.
Story Garden is a trademark of Publications International, Ltd.

One day mother pig told her three little pigs that it was time for them to go out into the world to make their own way.

The first little pig met a man with a bundle of straw. The pig bought some straw from the man and built his house with it.

Soon a wolf knocked at the door, saying, "Little pig! Little pig! Let me come in!"

"Not by the hair on my chinny chin chin!" squealed the pig.

"Then I'll huff, and I'll puff, and I'll blow your house in!" said the wolf.

The wolf huffed, and he puffed, and he blew the house in. He blew so hard that he blew the little pig away.

The second little pig bought sticks from the same man and built his house with them.

It wasn't long before the wolf came along. He knocked on the door, saying, "Little pig! Little pig! Let me come in!"

"Not by the hair on my chinny chin chin!" squealed the second little pig.

"Then I'll huff, and I'll puff, and I'll blow your house in!" threatened the wolf.

The wolf huffed, and he puffed, and he blew the house in. He blew so hard that he blew away the second little pig, too.

The third little pig met the same man and bought a load of bricks. This pig built a very sturdy house.

Soon the wolf was pounding on his door. "Little pig! Little pig! Let me come in!"

"Not by the hair on my chinny chin chin! squealed the third little pig.

"Then I'll huff, and I'll puff, and I'll blow your house in!" roared the wolf.

The wolf huffed, and he puffed, and he huffed and puffed some more, but he could not blow that little pig's house in.

The angry wolf made up his mind to have the third little pig for dinner. He thought up a plan. "Little pig," he said, "I know where there is a nice field of turnips."

"Where?" asked the little pig.

"At Farmer Brown's," said the wolf. "I'll pick you up at six o'clock tomorrow morning and take you there."

The little pig agreed. But he was too smart for the wolf. He got up at five o'clock in the morning, got the turnips, and was back in his house when the wolf arrived at six.

"Little pig, are you ready?" asked the wolf.

"Ready!" scoffed the pig. "I've already gone and come back with turnips for my dinner!"

The wolf was very angry that he had been tricked, but he tried again.

"Little pig," he said sweetly, "I know where there is a tree loaded with juicy apples."

"Where?" asked the pig.

"In Granny Smith's garden," said the wolf. "I'll come for you tomorrow at five o'clock in the morning. We will go together."

The little pig woke up at four o'clock and went off to find the apples. The wolf also got up at four o'clock. When the pig was not at home, the wolf went over to the apple tree.

The little pig was just about to come down from the tree with some apples when he saw the wolf below.

The little pig was very frightened. The wolf came close and called up to him, "My, you're up early. How are the apples?"

The pig thought quickly. "Delicious!" he said. "Why don't you stand back and I will throw one down to you."

The little pig tossed the apple as far as he could. He threw the apple so far that he came down the tree and was safely home before the wolf found it.

Back at his house, the pig made applesauce and apple pie, and he still had plenty of apples left to eat.

In the meantime, the wolf was furious that he had been tricked again. So, he thought up another plan.

The next day the wolf went over to the little pig's house and said, "Little pig, there is a fair in the town today. Let's go together! I'll come by for you at three this afternoon."

You will not be surprised that the clever pig started out early for the fair. He enjoyed all the sights and smells of the fair, but he didn't want to stay long. The little pig wanted to get home before the wolf showed up.

The little pig was on his way home with a barrel he had bought at the fair when he saw the wolf coming up the hill toward him.

The tricky little pig crawled into the barrel to hide. When he did, the barrel started rolling down the hill with the little pig in it.

The barrel rolled over and over, gathering speed on its way down the hill straight for the wolf. This strange sight frightened the wolf so much that he ran right home.

The wolf went to the little pig's house the next day. "Little pig," he said, "I was going to meet you at the fair yesterday, when the most frightening thing came rolling down the hill. I ran straight home!"

The little pig laughed. "Ha, ha! It was I that frightened you! I was in the barrel!"

The wolf was very angry when he learned that the little pig had frightened him so with the barrel. He made up his mind right then and there that he would eat the little pig for dinner that very day.

"Little pig," roared the wolf, "I am going to eat you for dinner today! I may not have been able to blow your house in or have been able to trick you, but I'm going to come down the chimney to get you now!"

With that the wolf leaped up on the roof. "Here I come, little pig!" he snarled down into the chimney.

But the smart little pig had hung a pot full of water over the fire. The wolf tumbled down the chimney right into the big pot of boiling water. The pig quickly put a heavy lid on the pot, and that was the end of the wolf.

The little pig lived happily ever after.